20 FUN FACTS ABOUT THE LEANING TOWER OF PISA

BY EMILY MAHONEY

Gareth Stevens
PUBLISHING

Please visit our website, www.garethstevens.com. For a free color catalog of all our high-quality books, call toll free 1-800-542-2595 or fax 1-877-542-2596.

Library of Congress Cataloging-in-Publication Data

Names: Mahoney, Emily Jankowski, author.
Title: 20 fun facts about the leaning Tower of Pisa / Emily Mahoney.
Other titles: Twenty fun facts about the Leaning Tower of Pisa
Description: New York : Gareth Stevens Publishing, [2020] | Series: Fun fact file: world wonders | Includes index.
Identifiers: LCCN 2018053821| ISBN 9781538237823 (pbk.) | ISBN 9781538237847 (library bound) | ISBN 9781538237830 (6 pack)
Subjects: LCSH: Leaning Tower (Pisa, Italy)–Juvenile literature. | Pisa (Italy)–Buildings, structures, etc.–Juvenile literature. | Pisa (Italy)–History–Juvenile literature. | Bell towers–Italy–Pisa–Juvenile literature.
Classification: LCC NA5621.P716 M34 2020 | DDC 720.945/551–dc23
LC record available at https://lccn.loc.gov/2018053821
First Edition

Published in 2020 by
Gareth Stevens Publishing
111 East 14th Street, Suite 349
New York, NY 10003

Designer: Sarah Liddell
Editor: Kristen Nelson

Photo credits: Cover, p. 1 D. Bond/Shutterstock.com; file folder used throughout David Smart/Shutterstock.com; binder clip used throughout luckyraccoon/Shutterstock.com; wood grain background used throughout ARENA Creative/Shutterstock.com; pp. 5, 16 Fedor Selivanov/Shutterstock.com; p. 6 Anette Andersen/Shutterstock.com; p. 7 agean/Shutterstock.com; p. 8 Mariano Regidor/Shutterstock.com; p. 9 Peter Hermes Furian/Shutterstock.com; p. 10 De Agostini/Biblioteca Ambrosiana/Getty Images; p. 11 Bettmann Contributor/Bettmann/Getty Images; p. 12 Bildagentur-online/Contributor/Getty Images; pp. 13, 14, 20 De Agostini Picture LIbrary/Contributor/De Agostini/Getty Images; p. 15 Martianmister and Vps/Wikimedia Commons; p. 18 Fesus Robert/Shutterstock.com; pp. 19, 21 Hulton Archive/Stringer/Hulton Archive/Getty Images; p. 22 MicheleB/Shutterstock.com; p. 23 LoneWolf1976/Wikimedia Commons; p. 24 Sailko/Wikimedia Commons; p. 25 Zoran Pajic/Shutterstock.com; p. 26 DAVID HECKER/Staff/DDP/Getty Images; p. 27 josefkubes/Shutterstock.com; p. 29 gorillaimages/Shutterstock.com.

Printed in the United States of America

CPSIA compliance information: Batch #CS19GS: For further information contact Gareth Stevens, New York, New York at 1-800-542-2595.

CONTENTS

Words in the glossary appear in **bold** type the first time they are used in the text.

A FAMOUS TILT

The Leaning Tower of Pisa is located in Pisa, a city in central Italy. Its construction began in 1173, and it took almost 200 years to finish—partly because of the tower's **tilt**.

Those who built the tower didn't plan on the tower leaning to one side. It's surprising they continued to build after noticing the problems during construction. Today, this leaning tower is considered one of the wonders of the world. You can't miss its now-famous lean!

The tower has amazed people for centuries with its odd tilt.

FUN FACT: 1

STOLEN TREASURE LED TO THE BUILDING OF THE LEANING TOWER OF PISA.

In 1063, troops from Pisa **sacked** the city of Palermo on the island of Sicily. They brought back wealth and treasures. The city's leaders wanted to show off these riches and the city's growing importance in Italy by building something grand.

This photograph shows Pisa as it is today.

The Square of Miracles—sometimes called the Field of Miracles—also included a large church called a cathedral, a **baptistery**, and a cemetery, as well as the bell tower.

THE LEANING TOWER OF PISA WAS SUPPOSED TO BE ONE OF THE TALLEST BELL TOWERS IN THE WORLD AT THE TIME.

The tower was the last building to be built in the Piazza dei Miracoli, or Square of Miracles. But problems during building slowed its construction.

PISA'S NAME COMES FROM THE GREEK WORD FOR "MARSHY LAND."

There was a warning to builders right in the name of the city! A marsh is a place with soft, wet ground. Pisa had soft soil made up of shells, fine sand, and clay. It wasn't great for large buildings.

WHERE IS PISA?

SLOVENIA

CROATIA

BOSNIA AND
HERZEGOVINA

PISA

LIGURIAN SEA

ARNO RIVER

ITALY

ADRIATIC SEA

TYRRHENIAN SEA

Pisa is found on the Arno River
close to the Ligurian Sea in Italy.
Being so close to water is likely
why the land was marshy.

THE NAME OF THE TOWER'S ORIGINAL ARCHITECT IS UNKNOWN.

Bonanno Pisano was one of the men who oversaw the beginning of construction, but he wasn't the one who planned the building! Historians do know that Tommaso Pisano was the architect who finished the work.

10

THE LEAN

THE TOWER LEANED ALMOST FROM THE BEGINNING.

Only three stories had been built when the tower began to lean noticeably in 1178.

The tower started leaning only 5 years into building. The soil underneath it was much too soft for such a large building. The tower also had a heavy **foundation** that wasn't built very deep into the ground.

WAR MAY HAVE SAVED THE TOWER FROM COLLAPSE.

When builders saw the tower was leaning on the south side, they tried to add features that would make up for the lean. Their weight made it worse! Luckily, war and other troubles stopped construction for almost 100 years.

The break in building allowed the soil to **compress** and probably saved the tower from completely falling over!

This photo shows work being done to strengthen the tower in 1928.

THE TOWER HASN'T ALWAYS LEANED SOUTH.

Many people have worked to correct the tower's lean. **Engineers** in the 13th century tried to build straight up to correct the lean. It just made the tower lean another way! It eventually leaned south again, as it does to this day.

When the Leaning Tower of Pisa was finally finished during the late 1300s, it was eight stories high. This was impressively tall for the time!

THE TOWER'S HEIGHT HAS CHANGED OVER TIME.

The tower may have been planned to reach just more than 196 feet (60 m). But as it has sunk and leaned, the tower is 183.3 feet (55.86 m) tall on the low side and 185.9 feet (56.67 m) on the high side.

ITALIAN DICTATOR BENITO MUSSOLINI MADE THE LEAN WORSE.

Mussolini was the dictator of Italy from 1925 to 1943.

Mussolini was bothered by the tower and wanted to fix it. He had workers drill holes in the base and fill them with a mixture of cement, sand, and water called mortar. It made the tower's base heavier—and the tower lean further!

15

THE TOWER ONCE LEANED 5.5 DEGREES, WHICH WAS EQUAL TO 15 FEET (4.6 M)!

In 1990, a project began to stop the tower from leaning so dangerously. Soil was removed from underneath the foundation of the tower. This reduced the lean of the tower by about 17 inches (43 cm) to about 4 degrees!

Once work was done in 2001, the tower continued to get straighter without more soil removal. In 2008, **sensors** on the tower showed it wasn't moving anymore.

THE TOWER'S LEAN

5.5°

4°

The tower's degree of lean is based on the perpendicular, or a line that is straight up and down.

Other parts of Italy have leaning towers, too! The tower at St. Stephen's church in Venice, Italy, leans almost as much as the famous tower in Pisa!

THE LEANING TOWER OF PISA ISN'T THE ONLY TILTED TOWER IN PISA.

Two other bell towers have a bit of lean due to being built on the soft soil of the area. The Church of St. Nicola has a leaning bell tower that was also built during the 1100s.

PART OF HISTORY

GALILEO MAY HAVE TESTED A SCIENTIFIC IDEA ON THE LEANING TOWER OF PISA!

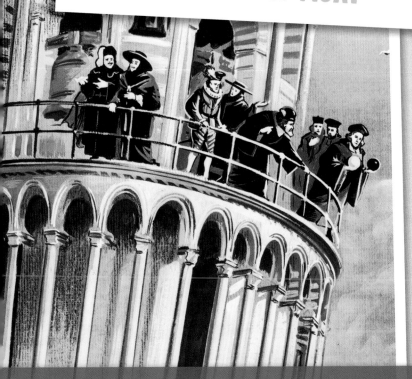

Some people aren't sure Galileo really did this experiment at all! He may have just written about what he thought would happen if he did.

Galileo Galilei was born in Pisa. He wrote about an **experiment** in which he dropped two balls of different weights from a tower to see what happened. He may have dropped them from the Leaning Tower of Pisa!

19

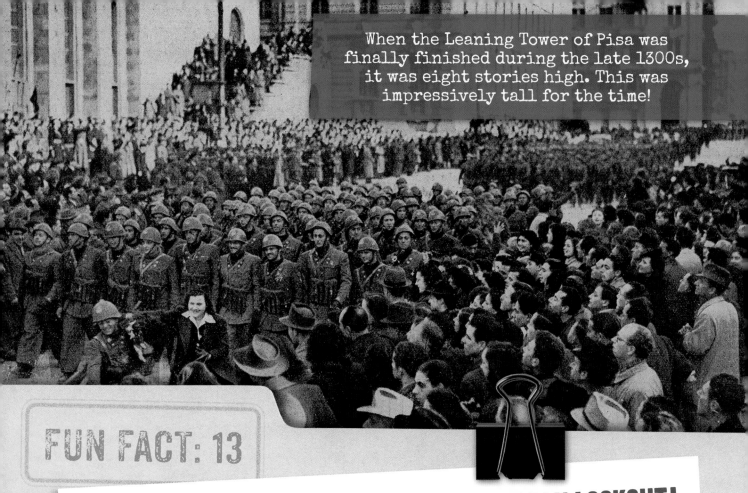

When the Leaning Tower of Pisa was finally finished during the late 1300s, it was eight stories high. This was impressively tall for the time!

THE TOWER MAY HAVE SERVED AS A GERMAN LOOKOUT!

Germany **occupied** Italy starting in 1943 during World War II (1939–1945). Being such a tall building in a coastal city, the Leaning Tower of Pisa may have been used by German troops to watch for enemies!

THE LEANING TOWER WAS ALMOST DESTROYED DURING WORLD WAR II.

This photo from 1944 shows the Leaning Tower of Pisa still standing, despite all of the destruction from World War II in other parts of Italy.

As American forces fought through Italy, they had orders to destroy buildings that could be used as German observation towers. They may have spared the Leaning Tower of Pisa for its beauty—or they may have had to **retreat** before they could finish the job!

21

THE TOWER TODAY

THE LEANING TOWER OF PISA WEIGHS MORE THAN 2,200 AFRICAN ELEPHANTS!

The tower is believed to weigh about 15,980 tons (14,500 mt). An African elephant can weigh as much as 7 tons (6.3 mt).

No wonder the tower sank into and leaned in the soft soil of Pisa!

The bells are still housed in the tower. The heaviest of these weighs almost 8,000 pounds (3,629 kg)!

THE TOWER'S BELLS HAVEN'T RUNG SINCE LAST CENTURY.

Seven very heavy bells were made for the bell chamber at the top of the tower. They aren't rung today, however. Engineers worried ringing them would cause the tower to lean even more.

STAIRCASES INSIDE THE TOWER DON'T HAVE THE SAME NUMBER OF STEPS.

One staircase has 294 steps. The other has two extra, making it 296 steps total. The extra steps make up for the building's lean! The staircases wind from the ground up to the bell chamber.

THE TOWER'S STAIRS ARE SAFE TO CLIMB.

The steps to the top of the tower are worn from the millions of visitors that have climbed them to the top over the years.

For a time, they were closed as the tower was made stronger. The years of work that have been done to the Leaning Tower of Pisa made it safe to climb the stairs inside. Many people do every year!

25

THE LEANING TOWER OF PISA ISN'T A RECORD HOLDER.

In 2007, the Guinness Book of World Records reported that

part of a church in Germany is the most tilted tower in the world!

Now that Pisa's tower only tilts about 4 degrees, the German

church's more than 5-degree lean gives it the record.

THE TOWER'S FUTURE

THE LEANING TOWER OF PISA IS STABLE—FOR NOW!

Engineers might have even better ways to strengthen the tower in 200 years!

Since 2008, the tower hasn't moved. Engineers think the tower could stay stable for about 200 years. But, after that, the soil might shift again and cause it to start leaning more once again!

27

STILL STANDING

For centuries, the Leaning Tower of Pisa has remained standing despite its well-known tilt. Some might view it as an an engineering mistake. But to stand for this long, something must have gone right at some point for this world wonder to be around today!

Are you brave enough to climb to the top of this tilted tower? Millions of visitors take in the beauty and history of the Leaning Tower of Pisa each year. You could be one of them!

Many visitors like to take pictures of themselves "holding up" the Leaning Tower of Pisa!

GLOSSARY

architect: a person who designs buildings

baptistery: a part of a church used for baptism, or an event in a Christian's life when they become a part of the church

collapse: to fall down or cave in

compress: to press or squeeze something so that it is smaller or fills less space

dictator: a person who rules a country with total authority

engineer: person who designs and builds things

experiment: a scientific test in which you carry out a series of actions and watch what happens in order to learn about something

foundation: the stone or concrete base that supports a building

occupy: to take and keep control of by using military power

retreat: the movement by soldiers away from the enemy because the enemy is winning or has won a battle

sack: to destroy and take things from a place, especially during a war

sensor: a tool that can detect changes in its surroundings

tilt: a slant, or something not straight up and down. Also, to be slanted.

FOR MORE INFORMATION

BOOKS

Furgang, Adam. *Engineering the Leaning Tower of Pisa*. Mankato, MN: Abdo Publishing, 2018.

Orr, Nicole K. *The Leaning Tower of Pisa*. Kennett Square, PA: Purple Toad Publishing, 2017.

WEBSITES

Facts About Leaning Tower of Pisa
www.dkfindout.com/us/earth/landmarks-world/leaning-tower-pisa/
Read more about the bell tower in Pisa and other cool landmarks.

Wonders of the World
www.kidsgen.com/wonders_of_the_world/
Read about more wonders of the world here.

INDEX